This Little Tiger book belongs to:

_____

_____

_____

For my good friend Paeony Lewis
~ D.B.

For Heidi, Chloe and Ben
for their love, support and cups of tea
~ D.H.

LITTLE TIGER PRESS
An imprint of Magi Publications
1 The Coda Centre, 189 Munster Road, London SW6 6AW
www.littletigerpress.com

First published in Great Britain 2003
by Little Tiger Press, London.
This edition published 2010

Text copyright © David Bedford 2003
Illustrations copyright © Magi Publications 2003
David Bedford has asserted his right
to be identified as the author and illustrator of this work
under the Copyright, Designs and Patents Act, 1988

ISBN 978-1-84895-182-2
Printed in China
2 4 6 8 10 9 7 5 3 1

What Are You Doing in My Bed?

Bed?

David Bedford

illustrated by Daniel Howarth

LITTLE TIGER PRESS

Kip the kitten had nowhere to sleep
on a dark and cold winter's night.
So he crept through a door . . .

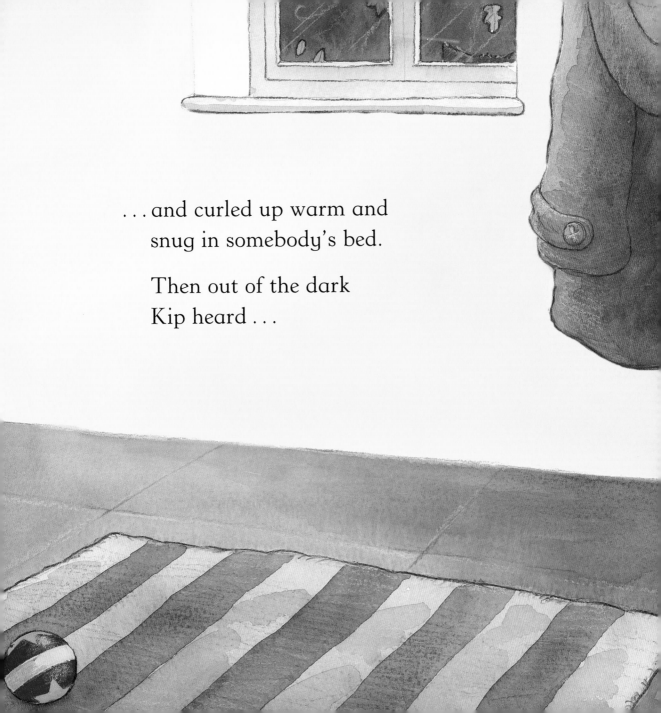

. . . and curled up warm and
snug in somebody's bed.

Then out of the dark
Kip heard . . .

. . . whispers and hisses,
and soft feet padding
through the night.

Bright green eyes peered
in through the window,
and suddenly . . .

. . . one, two, three, four, five, six cats
came banging through the cat door!
They tumbled and skidded and rolled
across the floor, where they found . . .

...Kip!
"What are YOU doing in OUR bed?"
shouted the six angry cats.

"Your bed?" said Kip.
"But this bed's too small for
    you. You'd never all fit!"

"Never fit?" said the cats.
"Just you watch . . ."

One, two, three cats curled up
neatly, head-to-tail . . .

then four, five, six cats
piled on top.

"See? There's no room for you," they said. "You'd never fit."

"Never fit?" said Kip. "Just you watch . . ."

Tottering and teetering,
  Kip carefully climbed on top.
"I'll sleep here," he said.

"OK," the cats yawned.
"But don't fidget or snore."
  And they fell asleep in a heap.

  But suddenly, a big, deep,
  growly voice said . . .

"WHAT ARE YOU DOING IN MY BED? SCRAM!"

The cats scattered around the room, but only found hard, cold places to sleep.

Harry the dog was comfy in his bed,
and he soon began to snore.

But then an icy wind whistled in
through the cat door, and Harry
awoke and shivered.

Kip whispered, "Follow me . . ."
and he quickly led six cold cats
across the floor . . .

. . . to the cozy bed.
"We'll keep you warm,"
said Kip.

"You'll never all fit," chattered Harry.
"Never fit?" said Kip. "Just you watch . . ."

Kip and Harry snored right through the night under their warm blanket of cats.

And they all fitted purr-fectly!

More fantastic reads from Little Tiger Press!

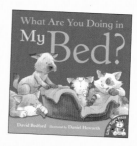

For information regarding any of the above titles or for our catalog, please contact us:
Little Tiger Press, 1 The Coda Centre, 189 Munster Road, London SW6 6AW, UK
Tel: +44 (0)20 7385 6333 • Fax: +44 (0)20 7385 7333 E-mail: info@littletiger.co.uk • www.littletigerpress.com